Rock Island Public Library
401 19th Street
Rock Island, IL 61201

MAR - - 2022

Teen Activism LIBRARY

STAND UP
for Animal Welfare

Jennifer Stephan

San Diego, CA

© 2022 ReferencePoint Press, Inc.
Printed in the United States

For more information, contact:
ReferencePoint Press, Inc.
PO Box 27779
San Diego, CA 92198
www.ReferencePointPress.com

ALL RIGHTS RESERVED.
No part of this work covered by the copyright hereon may be reproduced or used in any form or by any means—graphic, electronic, or mechanical, including photocopying, recording, taping, web distribution, or information storage retrieval systems—without the written permission of the publisher.

LIBRARY OF CONGRESS CATALOGING-IN-PUBLICATION DATA

Names: Stephan, Jennifer, author.
Title: Stand up for animal welfare / by Jennifer Stephan.
Description: San Diego, CA : ReferencePoint Press, Inc., 2022. | Series: Teen activism library | Includes bibliographical references and index.
Identifiers: LCCN 2021014911 (print) | LCCN 2021014912 (ebook) | ISBN 9781678201487 (library binding) | ISBN 9781678201494 (ebook)
Subjects: LCSH: Animal welfare--Juvenile literature.
Classification: LCC HV4708 .S655 2022 (print) | LCC HV4708 (ebook) | DDC 179/.3--dc23
LC record available at https://lccn.loc.gov/2021014911
LC ebook record available at https://lccn.loc.gov/2021014912

CONTENTS

Introduction   4
Teens Compelled to Act for Animal Welfare

Chapter One   8
The Issue Is Animal Welfare

Chapter Two   21
The Activists

Chapter Three   32
The Teen Activist's Tool Kit

Chapter Four   44
Risks and Rights

Source Notes   54
Where to Go for Ideas and Inspiration   57
Index   60
Picture Credits   64
About the Author   64

INTRODUCTION

Teens Compelled to Act for Animal Welfare

Circuses promise reality-bending feats of flight and fancy, but for teen activist Bella Lack, circus acts involving wild animals do not entertain. They exploit. In 2018, fifteen-year-old Lack learned that animals still performed in traveling circuses in the United Kingdom, where she lives. Images of camels and zebras contorted into cages, dragged from town to town, and forced to perform unnatural tricks for loud audiences propelled her into action. She took to social media to raise awareness and started an online petition to stop wild animal performances. "This is a heartbreaking and inhumane way to treat animals,"[1] wrote Lack on Change.org. Nearly two hundred thousand people signed the petition, and in July 2019, the teen declared victory. Bending under pressure from Lack and others, the UK government banned wild animals in circuses.

Teens Called to Action

Teen activists Genesis Butler and Zoe Rosenberg share Lack's passion for protecting the vulnerable. They stand up for the more than 9.6 billion animals killed in the United States annually for food. Other activists fight for pets stuck in abusive or neglectful homes and the estimated 6.5 million companion animals that face homelessness each year. Just like humans, many, if not all, animals experience pleasure and pain. Animals can be intelligent, curious, and social, but they cannot speak for themselves. So, activists speak out for those that lack necessities and suffer mistreatment.

For some teens, it is not just the suffering of animals that compels them to act but also the complacency of too many adults. Discussing threats of mass extinction and climate destruction, Lack asks, "Why on earth can we young people see the necessity to pour everything we have into fighting these crises when many of our leaders only think of enriching their lives in the present at the cost of the quality of life of future generations?"[2] Adults who fail to act also frustrate Genesis Butler, a teen activist who promotes veganism to improve animal welfare. "Adults are talking about [veganism] a little bit, but not as much as they should, so youth are stepping up and doing it,"[3] says Butler. Some detractors dismiss teen activists as meddling in grown-up business, but teens like Lack and Butler feel they have no choice but to act.

> "This is a heartbreaking and inhumane way to treat animals."[1]
>
> —Bella Lack, teen activist

Youth have been pushing aside curtains of ignorance and apathy throughout history. During the 1940s, for example, a group of German youth published and distributed leaflets calling out Nazi atrocities when many others stood silent. African American youth stood at the forefront of the civil rights movement during the 1950s and 1960s. During the 2010s, American Indigenous youth organized against an oil pipeline threatening their water supply, and survivors of the Marjory Stoneman Douglas High School shooting organized the March For Our Lives protest to stop gun violence. Among youth activists today stand those who feel called to fight against the often-ignored suffering of animals.

Animal rights activist Genesis Butler, thirteen, poses with rescued birds at a Southern California wildlife center in February 2020. Butler promotes a vegan diet as a strategy to improve animal welfare and address climate change.

Teen Power

Although teens do not have legislative or corporate power, they do have other powers. Teens bring new perspectives and ideas to activism. They have energy and passion, and their age can draw attention to their causes. Teens use digital tools and navigate digital spaces with expertise, which allows them to rapidly raise awareness, coordinate actions, and inspire other teens to get involved. Youth also have monetary power. Marketing firm Barkley estimates that Americans ages seven to twenty-one spend up to $143 billion a year themselves. Nearly all parents report that tweens and teens also influence household purchases. Tweens and young teens cannot vote, but they have power that can influence the products businesses sell, the policies governments adopt, and the choices individuals make.

Teen activism does not just have the potential to transform the lives of animals but also the lives of activists. While making change, activists can learn new skills, build meaningful social connections, and find a sense of purpose. Zoe Rosenberg even discovered courage through activism. Rosenberg draws attention to animal welfare through public displays. At age sixteen, she ran onto the field of the 2019 National Collegiate Athletic Association's football championship midgame to protest the treatment of chickens at the stadium's supplier. In front of nearly seventy-five thousand people, Rosenberg dodged roaring fans, cut through a tangle of cheerleaders and coaches, and unfurled a white protest banner as wide as her arms could reach. But bold action did not always come naturally to Rosenberg. "When I first became an animal rights activist at age eleven, I started behind a computer screen. . . . I didn't want to speak to anyone. . . . I was deeply afraid of confrontation. Eventually I realized that the animal rights movement wasn't about me, and that in the bigger picture my comfort zone didn't matter,"[4] she writes. Rosenberg's passion for helping farm animals led her to find new strength.

> "I started behind a computer screen. . . . I was deeply afraid of confrontation. Eventually I realized that the animal rights movement wasn't about me, and that in the bigger picture my comfort zone didn't matter."[4]
>
> —Zoe Rosenberg, teen activist

Animal welfare motivates teens like Lack, Butler, and Rosenberg. The power of working together for a good cause sustains their drive. And they hope their enthusiasm will encourage others—perhaps even you—to stand up for change.

CHAPTER ONE

The Issue Is Animal Welfare

Americans seem to love animals. They spend almost $100 billion a year on pets. In surveys, the vast majority of people say animal welfare is important. Yet billions of animals suffer, activists contend, for entertainment, profit, or just attention-grabbing selfies. Some animals lack necessities like a home, adequate supplies of food and water, time to bond with a mother, or basic medical treatment. Many endure cages that restrict movement and hardwired behaviors. Although laws protect endangered species and pets, almost none protect farm animals, and even protected animals can fall through legal loopholes or cracks in enforcement.

Animal welfare activists stand up for the voiceless. No matter the focus of their work—farm, wild, or companion animals—activists agree that too many animals suffer. Activists believe if people learn more about what animals endure, they will better align their actions with their feelings.

Going Undercover on a Dairy Farm

According to the Vegetarian Resource Group, about 3 percent of Americans eat a vegan diet—no meat, dairy, or eggs. Everyone else has some connection to farm animals. Animal welfare activists want people to better understand the origin of their meals. That knowledge can be disturbing.

Videos taken by activists working undercover on farms show grim conditions and mistreatment.

On June 4, 2019, the Animal Recovery Mission (ARM) released undercover video taken at Fair Oaks Farms in Indiana. Part working dairy farm and part tourist attraction, Fair Oaks promises its customers happy cows and "A Dairy Good Time for the Family."[5] In one Fair Oaks ad, a young employee dressed in overalls strokes the head of a calf as she feeds him a bottle of milk. The undercover video shot at the dairy's calf care facility just up the road also shows calves being bottle-fed. But instead of stroking, there is shoving and smacking. Staff with hair-trigger tempers lash out at newborns that resist or struggle to take a bottle.

ARM's agent captured these feeding scenes and other daily routines using a hidden mic and camera. He got a job at the calf care facility and worked there undercover for three months. Just hours after birth, calves arrive at the facility, where hundreds of huts spread across a field in rows and columns as orderly as graph paper. In ARM's video, staff deliver each calf—sometimes violently—into a separate plastic hut far from its bellowing mother. Workers drive the grassless rows, stopping to brand new arrivals and provide milk. Carrying out daily chores, these employees drag and push the newborns. The injured do not receive medical attention. The images are heartbreaking.

ARM knew the video would grab the public's attention. Indeed, ARM counted on it. In the glare of public scrutiny, Fair Oaks promised to improve. The employees caught on camera were fired, although some had been fired before the video's release. Fairlife, the producer of Fair Oaks' milk, and Coca-Cola, its distributor, scrambled to give press statements. Several retailers also reacted quickly. The "animal abuse in the Fair Oaks Farm network is chilling,"[6] said a spokesperson from Family Express, a chain of convenience stores in Indiana. They pulled Fairlife milk from their shelves, as did some other regional chains.

Law enforcement reacted less enthusiastically. The sheriff arrested one Fair Oaks employee, but charges were later dropped.

The response did not surprise ARM. "Arrests and charges brought are usually to please the media and the public," Richard Couto, ARM's founder, told a reporter. "Change will come from the consumer, not the courts."[7] The fact is, farm animals have few legal protections. The Animal Welfare Act, the main federal law that protects animals, excludes farm animals. All states have anticruelty laws, but most exempt common farming practices such as separating newborns from their mothers and confining them in small enclosures.

> "Arrests and charges brought are usually to please the media and the public. . . . Change will come from the consumer, not the courts."[7]
>
> —Richard Couto, founder of the Animal Recovery Mission

Animals on Factory Farms

Although the Fair Oaks abuse seems extreme, farm animals can also suffer from typical farming practices, according to activists. Today, most meat, dairy, and eggs come from large farms run like factories instead of small family farms. In the United States, over 9.6 billion land animals are slaughtered each year for food. Cows produce more than 25 billion gallons of milk, and hens lay 98 million eggs for consumption. The factory farm system produces large quantities of food quickly, but efficient production is not necessarily humane production.

A typical egg-producing farm in the United States houses at least seventy-five thousand chickens, some in buildings as long as football fields. These chicken houses reek with ammonia fumes from excrement and rumble with industrial fans. Most egg-laying hens, called layers, live their entire lives in cages so small they cannot extend their wings. Layers cannot scratch in dirt or roost, which are natural chicken behaviors. Chickens can get tangled in cage wire and, unable to reach their food or water, die. Eight states restrict the use of cages, but problems remain. Many cage-free layers never go outside. Farmers routinely cut off the ends of chickens' beaks so they will not peck at each other in overcrowded spaces. When a layer's egg production falls, she is killed.

Broiler chickens, grown for meat, can also suffer. They are typically raised in enormous, crowded barns. The average broiler farm sells over 270,000 chickens a year according to the US Department of Agriculture (USDA). For broilers, it is not small cages that prevent movement. Instead, they are bred to provide the maximum amount of sellable meat in the shortest amount of time. As they grow, broilers' muscles become too heavy for their bones, and they struggle to move. Broilers typically go to processors after just forty-seven days.

Other farm animals endure mistreatment too. On most dairy farms, cows are dehorned, repeatedly impregnated to keep up milk supplies, and separated from their young at birth. Forty states allow farmers to house sows in crates so small they cannot turn around.

One activist group secretly shot video that it said showed staff members mistreating cows at Fair Oaks Farms in Indiana. Pictured here are Fair Oaks cows on automatic milking machines.

Factory Farming for Profit

Farmers can raise animals more humanely. Some farmers let animals spend time outdoors and with their young. Some raise slow-grow chickens, which take longer to mature but lead more comfortable lives. These approaches, however, increase farmers' costs. Although some small farmers find customers willing to pay more for products raised humanely, that is not the operating model of factory farms.

To maximize profits, factory farms aim to produce large quantities of meat, milk, or eggs for the lowest cost. Packing and stacking layers means more eggs can hatch more cheaply. A short time to slaughter means a farm can produce more broilers per year. The constant impregnation of cows ensures big quantities of milk, and small crates mean more pigs can be raised in the same amount of space. Practices and conditions vary, but activists say factory farming typically maximizes profits at the expense of animal welfare.

Unless consumers or policy makers demand better treatment for farm animals, there is little incentive for factory farms to

On many farms, chickens live in crowded conditions. A few states restrict the use of cages, but even then many chickens are never allowed outdoors.

The Agricultural Industry Fights Back Against Undercover Activists

Farming is big business in Iowa, which is a top producer of eggs and pork. Iowa's agricultural industry employs about one out of every six Iowans directly or indirectly, and it generates $72.1 billion a year for the state's economy. That is a lot of jobs, a lot of tax revenue, and, consequently, a lot of political power for farmers.

Many of those farmers do not like undercover videos. Agricultural industry organizations say videos from animal welfare groups are misleading and could harm their businesses. In 2020, Iowa passed an "ag-gag" law that would stop undercover work. It is a tactic many farm states have tried. Ag-gag laws aim to punish undercover investigators or whistleblowers who expose what goes on at farms.

Activists believe the videos are critical for improving animal welfare and argue that ag-gag laws are unconstitutional and dangerous. "The mere existence of these laws is harmful," Animal Legal Defense Fund attorney Matthew Liebman told *VegNews*, "because they prevent people from engaging in protected free speech, chilling our constitutional rights before we even exercise them."

Courts in Iowa have dismissed two earlier versions of ag-gag laws. Factory farms hope the third time is the charm.

Quoted in Anna Starostinetskaya, "5 Quotes from the Man Who Helped Overturn Idaho's Ag-Gag Law," *VegNews*, August 5, 2015. https://vegnews.com.

---

change. Organizations such as ARM take undercover videos because they believe raising awareness will help change customers' minds and ultimately improve life for farm animals.

Wild Animals for Pets

It is not just farm animals that suffer confinement in small enclosures, separation of newborns from mothers, and other mistreatment, activists say. Although wild animals have more legal protections than farm animals, legal gaps and problematic enforcement make them vulnerable. No one knows exactly how many wild animals live in captivity, but more tigers reportedly live in the United States than anywhere in the wild. That is just one species. According to animal welfare activists, wild animals endure miserable conditions in homes as exotic pets or at wildlife attractions like roadside zoos.

The Performing Animal Welfare Sanctuary (PAWS) in California shares stories of its rescued animals to show what life can be like in captivity. Several of its residents are former pets, including Owen the bobcat. Authorities rescued Owen from a small, filthy cage in a family's backyard. Bobcats hunt prey as large as deer, run up to 30 miles per hour (42 kmh), and jump as far as 12 feet (4 m). Confining Owen to a small cage made it impossible for him to follow his instincts. A veterinary exam showed that Owen had chronic disease and debilitating arthritis, likely the result of malnutrition and inbreeding, according to the vet. Zeppo and Chico joined Owen at PAWS. They were two of fifty malnourished capuchin monkeys living as pets among piles of feces. Boo Boo the bear, also purchased as a pet, lives at PAWS with them. His owners locked a chain around his neck and then lost the key. As the bear grew, the chain embedded into his neck. After his rescue, a vet surgically removed the chain. The stories of the PAWS residents are not unique. According to activists, too many exotic pets suffer in small cages, unhygienic conditions, and with untreated medical issues.

Keeping exotic pets can lead to problems because owners often do not understand the needs of wild animals. The costs of care can be overwhelming. Small primates require about eight thousand dollars per year for care, and big cats cost about eighteen thousand dollars per year. The expense can mean some owners cut back on nutrition or medical attention. Problems also arise when cuddly babies turn into unruly adolescents that can tear apart a house or hurt people. To control these natural behaviors, owners often cage them. That is problematic too. "Without the opportunity to express normal, wild behaviors for which they are genetically programmed," PAWS explains, wild animals "can suffer."[8]

Elephants and Tigers for Entertainment

Other exotic animals in captivity live at animal attractions such as aquariums, zoos, and circuses. Conditions vary depending on the facility and species, but activists have spoken out most loudly for elephants and tigers.

Breaking Up Illegal Dog Fighting

A small number of animals endure extreme abuse in illegal animal fighting rings. The story of the bust of one such ring shows how they suffer. Early on October 10, 2019, New York police raided the homes of men allegedly involved in a dogfighting ring. Inside, as photos from the scene show, dogs peered out from wooden and metal cages stacked three high and four wide. Grime-splattered treadmills modified with wooden walls and a chain to attach a collar showed the dogs had no choice about exercise. Police found twenty-nine dogs that day. They seized weighted dog vests, used to develop thick muscles and stamina, and found breaking sticks, used to dislodge the jaws of one dog from the body of another. Looking at the conditions, it is easy to imagine the caged dogs would turn violent, but they were not born that way. Trainers forced them to be aggressive for entertainment and profit. That October morning, the American Society for the Prevention of Cruelty to Animals assisted the police. Their photos show the rescued dogs propped calmly in the arms of staff or waiting in carriers for transport to a better future.

In the wild, elephants live in family groups and roam up to 50 miles (80 km) a day. Under pressure from activists, many city zoos, concerned they cannot provide suitable habitats, have relocated elephants to sanctuaries or are phasing them out of the zoos' exhibits. The PAWS residents include former zoo elephant Maggie, who arrived in 2007 on a US Air Force cargo plane. She had lived in a small enclosure at the Alaska Zoo since childhood, alone for the last ten years. After she collapsed on the floor twice—it took firefighters and zookeepers over seven hours each time to lift her back up—the zoo responded to public outcries and let Maggie move to California.

Activists say that conditions at unaccredited wildlife attractions, so called roadside zoos, can be much worse. About twenty-five hundred animal exhibitors operate in the United States without accreditation from the Association of Zoos and Aquariums. Animals at roadside zoos often endure cramped spaces, malnutrition, and physical and psychological abuse.

At roadside zoos, tiger cubs are like ATMs. Thousands of people buy tickets for a chance to pet or bottle-feed a fuzzy cub.

Female tigers are forced to continuously produce litters, and then newborns are quickly snatched from their mothers for visitors to cuddle and photograph. At four months old, cubs retire. They become new cogs in the breeding cycle, are put on display, or, in some cases, are simply killed. The mistreatment happens merely for the sake of profit. According to journalist Sharon Guynup, "Cub-petting venues run on tourist dollars, exploiting one of the planet's most iconic, majestic animals strictly for the financial gain of a few individuals."[9] The plight of captive wild cats has even caught the attention of Congress, which is considering legislation to protect them.

The Wildlife Trade

Elephants, tigers, primates, and bears are not the only wild animals living in captivity. Some wild birds, reptiles, and amphibians also live as pets or at roadside zoos. Where do all the exotic animals in the United States come from? Some are bred in captivity. Others are abducted from the wild, sometimes squeezed in luggage or stuffed under clothes for undetected transport. That can lead to problems for an entire species. Wildlife traders have nearly depleted the African gray parrot and Madagascar's radiated tortoise populations. Wild animals that survive transit often get sold at pet fairs, on websites, or through social media platforms, including Facebook. Illegal wildlife trafficking is big business, generating $8.5 billion a year, according to the World Bank.

Laws to protect wild animals living in captivity have shortcomings. The federal Endangered Species Act regulates the ownership and trade of endangered species, but species identified by conservationists as threatened do not immediately gain legal protections. One study found it took an average of six to fourteen years for wild animals to make it onto the US endangered species list, depending on type of animal. The federal Animal Welfare Act provides minimum standards for exhibiting, breeding, and selling some animals, but it does not cover reptiles and amphibians. States can have stricter laws. Twenty states have comprehensive bans on the private possession or sale of exotic animals, but nineteen states do not require more than a license or permit to keep one. Even with laws on ownership and trade, small fines and scanty enforcement may offer little deterrence.

Exotic animals kept captive for entertainment or as pets can suffer. Some of the lucky ones eventually end up at a sanctuary such as PAWS, which extends over 2,300 acres (931 ha) of land and provides round-the-clock care to residents. Sanctuary animals do not perform for spectators, and like all true sanctuaries, PAWS does not breed. Still, the founders know it is not ideal. "All I can do is make their prison as comfortable as possible,"[10] said Patricia Derby, the late PAWS cofounder. According to Derby, wildlife belongs in the wild, but her rescued animals could not survive if they were returned there.

> "All I can do is make their prison as comfortable as possible."[10]
>
> —Patricia Derby, cofounder of the Performing Animal Welfare Society

Homeless Pets

Unlike wild animals, companion animals—such as cats and dogs—do belong in homes. The problem, according to activists, is that too many do not have homes. According to the American Society for the Prevention of Cruelty to Animals (ASPCA), about 6.5 million companion animals end up in shelters each year, and just around 3.2 million get adopted. The number of homeless pets has fallen dramatically over the last decades, but for activists, it remains too high.

Some animals come to shelters as strays. Others come from families who surrender pets. "Too many animals enter the shelter system for reasons that are completely preventable,"[11] says

> "Too many animals enter the shelter system for reasons that are completely preventable."[11]
>
> —Matt Bershadker, president of the American Society for the Prevention of Cruelty to Animals

Matt Bershadker, the president and chief executive officer of the ASPCA. Research finds that the most typical reason for surrendering a pet to a shelter is a pet's behavioral or health problems. Misconceptions about a pet's cost and needs can also lead to more animals entering shelters.

Animals who cannot find homes risk being euthanized. Shelters euthanize about 1.5 million a year. Like intake rates, euthanization rates have dropped dramatically over the last several decades. In a 2019 study, *New York Times* reporter Alicia Parlapiano found euthanasia rates had dropped over 75 percent in big city shelters since 2009. In 1971, the Los Angeles municipal shelter euthanized, on average, 300 animals per day, for example, but in 2018, just 10 animals per day. This decline has resulted from increased spay and neuter rates, programs to help owners afford to keep their pets, and an increase in shelter adoptions. Yet although intake and euthanasia rates have fallen, that does not comfort the millions of companion animals that remain homeless or the activists who fight for them.

Puppy Mills

Adoptions from shelters decrease pet homelessness, but just about 30 percent of pets come from a shelter or rescue. Some others come from reputable breeders, which generally sell on a small scale and work directly with families, but other dogs and cats come from pet stores or websites supplied by "puppy mills" or "kitten farms." These commercial breeding operations typically sell in large quantities and, by definition, keep animals in poor conditions.

An estimated ten thousand puppy mills operate in the United States, according to the Humane Society of the United States. Undercover investigations by animal welfare organizations reveal heartbreaking conditions. Female dogs are forced to breed, are separated from their pups at around eight weeks, and then are forced to breed again in a constant cycle. Videos show dogs with filth-matted fur yapping and whimpering in small cages. Feces

Millions of dogs, cats, rabbits, and other companion animals end up in shelters every year. Some are strays; others are given up by their owners.

and urine stain surfaces. For a few dogs, the stress is too much, and they spin frantically in circles in their cages. Puppy mills that cut corners in care do so to reduce costs and increase profits. The federal Animal Welfare Act sets minimum standards for breeders, but welfare organizations say they are insufficient, and monitoring is sparse.

Many puppies leave mills and the stores that sell them healthy, but not all escape unscathed. Some arrive at pet stores sick because of inbreeding or diseases that can spread easily in unhygienic or cramped spaces in mills or on transport trucks. Buyers enamored with wiggly puppies may not realize their condition. Owners who later confront unexpected vet bills or behavioral problems can feel overwhelmed. Some then leave their new pets at shelters, which exacerbates the homelessness problem.

Activists working with companion animals have achieved many successes. In addition to decreases in shelter and euthanization rates, the number of pet stores selling puppies from mills has declined. Some pet stores even partner with local shelters to match pets with families. Increased awareness may account for some of these positive changes. As people learn more about the realities of pet ownership and the origins of pet store pets, they can make better choices. The ASPCA's Bershadker believes that increased awareness about puppy mills has also changed attitudes about shelter adoptions. "Rescuing an animal has become a badge of honor,"[12] he told a *New York Times* reporter. Activists want to continue making progress for companion animals.

Animal Welfare Challenges

Most Americans say they care about animals. Some seek out products or experiences labeled *humane*. But the terms *cage-free*, *sanctuary*, and *USDA-licensed breeder* do not always mean what they seem like they should. Animals can suffer from people's misconceptions. Social media can perpetuate problems by driving demand for wow-inducing pets, unusual wildlife experiences, or adorable pet store puppies. Social media also provides a poorly regulated marketplace to trade animals, sometimes obscuring their origins or legal status. Agencies charged with law enforcement lack resources, and activists say laws leave animals vulnerable. According to activists, too many animals suffer from mistreatment. And whereas the large numbers of farm animals living in poor conditions motivate some activists, the degradation of wild species or the heartbreak of seeing pets suffer compels others.

CHAPTER TWO

The Activists

Together, animal welfare activists weave a safety net for all kinds of animals in all kinds of circumstances. Whereas some focus on wild animals, others advocate for companion or farm animals. Some activists believe reducing meat and dairy consumption helps animals. Others believe there is no way to use animal products ethically. Activists' strategies sometimes overlap, but as the following descriptions show, the activists have a core set of strategies they use frequently. The young activists who stand up for animal welfare have different interests, philosophies, and strategies but the same goal.

Mercy For Animals

Nathan Runkle grew up on a John Deere tractor in rural Ohio. For more than four generations, his family had farmed. Farming seemed like Runkle's destiny too. Then, at age fifteen, a bucket of piglets headed for dissection changed his life. When one frightened piglet arrived at school still alive, a student slammed it onto the concrete floor to kill it. The bloodied piglet survived. A horrified teacher rushed the animal to the vet, but the baby pig could not be saved. In the end, the student did not get punished because "thumping" pigs is standard farming practice. Instead, the teacher who tried to help the piglet was asked to resign. "I saw a real injustice," Runkle recalls, "and I knew if this had been a puppy or a kitten that this had happened to, it would have likely been national news."[13] Soon after, Runkle started Mercy For Animals.

Now, over twenty years later, Mercy For Animals is known for its undercover videos. Undercover investigators risk their physical and mental health to gain leverage in the fight to improve animal welfare. After training in how to gather evidence, investigators seek jobs on farms suspected of inhumane practices. Once hired, they record daily routines with a hidden camera. It is a dangerous, difficult job. Investigators leave friends and family to move temporarily to job locations. They must convincingly inhabit made-up personas and work under the fear of detection. During the day, investigators work physically demanding and heart-wrenching jobs. At night, they build cases with notes. In the end, an investigator can scrape manure off his or her shoes and shower off dirt and dust, but the images of cruelty last. Investigators can suffer from nightmares, anxiety, or depression. Still, they choose the job because of the potential impact of video evidence. "I believe the most powerful tool in the war for truth is the video camera," says Kevin Lahey, a former Mercy For Animals investigator. "How can one argue with footage?"[14]

> "I believe the most powerful tool in the war for truth is the video camera. How can one argue with footage?"[14]
>
> —Kevin Lahey, a former undercover investigator for Mercy For Animals

Undercover videos can lead to criminal charges, but in many cases they do not. Standard farming practices are typically legal. Local law enforcement can have close ties with farmers in their area. In some instances, law enforcement even turns against the investigators rather than pursuing the perpetrators. Mercy For Animals investigators do not take big risks for a chance to send a few animal abusers to jail. Instead, their videos aim to inflame the public and ignite policy change. Videos can spark individuals to make more humane choices about what they eat and where they shop. They can also motivate new people to become activists. Impas-

In 2008, a few years after founding Mercy for Animals, Nathan Runkle speaks to the media about a video his group shot at a California egg farm. The video shows workers mistreating chickens. It also shows cages so small that the birds cannot spread their wings.

sioned consumers and constituents then pressure companies and politicians to enact new policies or legislation that will improve animal welfare. Video is so powerful that sometimes the threat of a release is enough to change a company's policy.

Mercy For Animals has conducted over seventy investigations and has helped change policies at companies, including Nestlé, McDonald's, and Perdue. The organization has also helped pass legislation in Ohio, California, and Colorado to improve farm animal welfare.

Students Opposing Speciesism

Students Opposing Speciesism (SOS) is a youth-led group within People for the Ethical Treatment of Animals (PETA), an organiza-

Fundraising for the Blue-Footed Booby

Bella Lack is not the only teen fundraising for wildlife. In fifth grade, Will Gladstone learned that blue-footed boobies, birds famous for their blue feet, were in trouble. Their population in the Galápagos Islands had fallen dramatically. Will decided to help, and he enlisted his brother Matthew too. In 2016, they started the Blue Feet Foundation. The foundation sells aqua-colored socks featuring a waddling bird to help raise conservation funds for the blue-footed booby.

Despite the brothers' enthusiasm, the launch of their foundation hit the ground with a thud. It took them three months to sell their first pair of socks. Instead of giving up, they came up with a marketing plan. The brothers set up an Instagram account and reached out to local celebrities who had demonstrated an interest in animals. Their efforts paid off. The brothers, now sixteen and thirteen, have sold over twenty thousand pairs and have raised more than $150,000 for research. "They literally created this lemonade stand on steroids," their father told the *Christian Science Monitor*.

Quoted in Riley Robinson, "Saving the Blue-Footed Booby, One Pair of Socks at a Time," *Christian Science Monitor*, November 13, 2019. www.csmonitor.com.

---

tion founded in 1980. SOS and PETA believe that humans and animals have equal value. "If you wouldn't eat a dog, a cat, or your annoying uncle, then the only reason you're eating a pig is because of speciesism,"[15] says SOS member Krystal Gates. Speciesism is the belief that the human species is superior to other species, and SOS thinks it is unethical.

Launched in March 2020, SOS has over one thousand youth members in the United States and Canada. They work to protect all kinds of animals. The SOS Instagram account documents the group's efforts to abolish the use of animals in products, research, and school dissections. Like other activists, SOS and PETA believe animal welfare improves when individuals pressure corporate and government policy makers for change. SOS draws attention to animal cruelty and encourages individuals to protest, petition, share photos and videos, and boycott businesses and organizations.

SOS is a new organization, but PETA has a long, controversial history of activism. It is known for its campaigns and extreme methods. Past tactics include displaying posters with graphic images of animal cruelty, spray-painting the office of a fashion designer, crashing fashion runways, and throwing tofu pies. One of their most famous campaigns, the "I'd Rather Go Naked" antifur campaign, features mostly naked celebrities (strategically covered up) to protest clothing made from real fur.

Recently, PETA has begun to change its tactics. Before social media, PETA used shocking images and displays to grab attention. "We would work very hard to get an eight-second clip from one of our videos on the news at night," Tracy Reiman, the executive vice president at PETA, told a *New York Times* reporter. "Now we'll put it on Facebook or Instagram, and millions of people will see it within 24 hours."[16] These days, PETA uses social media to quickly win fights. It has had many successes in changing consumer behavior and corporate policies as well as in helping to pass legislation.

Young activists in Netherlands promote climate-change awareness during a 2019 climate change protest. Youth-led groups like this one have been instrumental in bringing attention to issues like climate change and animal welfare around the world.

Genesis Butler

At age three, Genesis Butler learned that chicken nuggets come from dead chickens. She became a vegetarian. At age six, Butler learned that the milk she drank came from mother cows. She became vegan. She then converted her family into vegans. Now, Butler is thirteen and working to get the rest of the world on board.

Butler promotes a vegan diet as a strategy to improve animal welfare and address climate change. Factory farms account for a significant amount of greenhouse gas emissions. Butler also believes eliminating factory farms is a matter of social justice. In North Carolina, for example, factory farms are disproportionately located in communities of color or low-income communities. Animal waste, sometimes collected in lagoons of excrement, can pollute water and air and threaten people's physical and mental health and their quality of life.

The teen activist, who identifies as Black, Mexican, and Indigenous, also works to dispel inaccurate stereotypes of vegans. "I think veganism is thought of as a white thing or thing for hippies to do, but it's not," Butler explained to a journalist. "There are people of all races and backgrounds who are vegan."[17]

Butler promotes veganism through talks and social media. At age ten, she became one of the youngest people to give a TEDx talk. On social media, she shares information about animal welfare, vegan products, and meal ideas with around seventy thousand followers. She donates her speaking fees and raises money through her nonprofit, Genesis for Animals, to support sanctuary animals. Recently, the teen has started Youth Climate Save to organize more youth activists in promoting plant-based diets.

For her work, Butler has received multiple awards, including PETA's 2019 Young Animal Activist of the Year and the Sir Paul

> "I think veganism is thought of as a white thing or thing for hippies to do, but it's not. . . . There are people of all races and backgrounds who are vegan."[17]
>
> —Genesis Butler, teen activist

The Animal Legal Defense Fund Adopts a Creative Legal Strategy

When the Animal Recovery Mission released undercover video in 2019 exposing animal abuse at Fair Oaks Farms dairy, the sheriff arrested one person, but the charges were later dropped. Lawyers from the Animal Legal Defense Fund (ALDF) and other organizations believe the companies involved should not be allowed to dodge justice so easily. With few laws to protect farm animals, the attorneys have gotten creative. Consumer protection laws protect people from lies in advertising. The ALDF and other law firms have filed a class action lawsuit against Fairlife, the producer of Fair Oaks' milk, alleging deceptive advertising. Fairlife claimed its cows were treated with "extraordinary care." The ALDF disagrees, and its lawyers think a jury that sees video of the abuse will disagree too. If a jury rules that Fairlife has defrauded customers with its claims, other companies may have an incentive to improve animal welfare policies too. The case was still pending in early 2021.

Quoted in Robert Channick, "Fairlife Milk Faces Potentially Massive Class Action Lawsuit," *Chicago Tribune*, November 27, 2019. https://digitaledition.chicagotribune.com.

McCartney Young Veg Advocate award from the group Animal Hero Kids. She has also been featured in an episode of the Disney+ *Marvel Hero Project* and in two American Girl books.

The American Society for the Prevention of Cruelty to Animals

The American Society for the Prevention of Cruelty to Animals (ASPCA) focuses on improving the welfare of companion animals such as dogs, cats, and horses. Its programs aim to prevent homelessness, enable adoptions of shelter pets, rescue pets from abuse, and help enforce and enact laws. Many young people volunteer to assist in these services.

The ASPCA has long worked to prevent pet homelessness. It sponsors pet food banks and provides money to pet owners in financial need to help with veterinarian bills or apartment pet deposits. The ASPCA also offers free or low-cost spaying and neutering so that unwanted litters will not be left on the streets. When the COVID-19 pandemic hit in 2020, many families struggled to pay bills. For some, keeping a pet became difficult. So, the ASPCA committed $5 million to help pet owners and organizations like shelters keep animals safe and healthy.

For companion animals that do end up in shelters, ASPCA programs help to get them adopted. The ASPCA's relocation programs help even out supply and demand across shelters nationwide. Whereas some shelters may have room for more animals, others buckle under an oversupply, which can lead to high euthanization rates. In 2019, the organization relocated more than forty-two thousand pets from southern regions in the United States to midwestern and northern states. Working with Wings of Rescue, the ASPCA also helps relocate shelter animals impacted by hurricanes.

To improve the lives of animals that live in abusive situations—such as puppy mills, dogfighting rings, or with neglectful pet owners—the ASPCA works with law enforcement and legislators. Staff members gather forensic evidence, rescue animals, provide veterinary help and temporary shelter, and support policing and prosecutions by providing specialized knowledge. Its experience on the front lines of rescues and homelessness also allows the ASPCA to speak knowledgeably to legislators. The organization advocates for new laws to improve animal welfare.

Since its founding in 1866, the ASPCA has had a significant impact on the welfare of companion animals. In 2019, the organization stated that it had been involved in seven rescues; had relocated over forty-two thousand animals; had spayed or neutered more than seventy-three thousand animals; and, in Los Angeles alone, had distributed fifty-five thousand pounds of dog and cat food.

Bella Lack and Reserva

At age eleven, Bella Lack saw a video showing the devastating effects of the palm oil industry on the orangutan population. Moved by the struggle of these long-haired apes, Lack plastered her house with posters and gave a school presentation to inform classmates. She quickly figured out that social media was a much more effective medium for her message.

At age fifteen, Lack traveled to Thailand to investigate elephants in the tourism trade. Tourists can ride into the jungle on the backs of the pachyderms, watch them perform tricks, or pose wrapped in their trunks. However, there is nothing natural about elephants throwing darts or painting pictures. Trainers use chains, spikes, and bull hooks to instill these behaviors. To raise awareness, Lack shot and posted video to YouTube exposing the mistreatment.

In 2020, Lack cofounded the youth council of Reserva: The Youth Land Trust. Reserva uses the energy of youth and the power of social media to raise money to set aside land in the Ecuadorian rain forest. Habitat destruction has devastated this area, which is home to many endangered species. The foundation raises awareness about the threat of extinction, raises funds for the reserve, and encourages youth to fundraise and write letters to policy makers. "What really excites me about Reserva," Lack said in an interview with conservationist and reporter Lizzie Daly "is that it's an opportunity for young people to take concrete action. We're not here just to protest. We're actually here to provide a space for young people who want to recognize their power in a different way."[18] Reserva, in partnership with the Rainforest Trust, has funded 157 of 244 acres of rain forest so far. After completing the first phase, the foundation will raise funds to protect another 976 acres in the Dracula Youth Reserve.

Today, the seventeen-year-old British activist works with multiple animal welfare organizations to bring attention to the struggles of wild animals and fundraising for their protection. "Although one individual action won't save the world," Lack writes, "the accumulated actions of a unified community can impact political, social and economic structures."[19] Lack motivates people to action through her talks and writing. She has spoken at the Illegal Wildlife Trade Conference in 2018 and on the TEDx Talk stage. She has written for British *Vogue*, tweets regularly to more

> "Although one individual action won't save the world, the accumulated actions of a unified community can impact political, social and economic structures."[19]
>
> —Bella Lack, teen activist

than 140,000 Twitter followers, and will soon release her first book about youth activism. Lack also is completing a documentary film with primatologist Jane Goodall.

Despite her young age, or perhaps because of it, Lack seems to have made an impact on animal welfare. She helped pass a ban on the use of wild animals in circuses in the United Kingdom, shined a spotlight on the illegal ivory trade, and is protecting animals in the Ecuadorian rain forest. Lack is also a youth ambassador for the Born Free Foundation, Save the Asian Elephants, the Jane Goodall Institute, and the Royal Society for the Prevention of Cruelty to Animals.

The Animal Legal Defense Fund

The Animal Legal Defense Fund (ALDF) improves animal welfare using the legal system, and many of its fights occur in court. The ALDF has sued neglectful and abusive pet owners, roadside zoo operators, breeders, and farms. Sometimes these cases involve creative legal strategies, alleging fraud or public nuisance when laws specifically addressing mistreatment are weak. In 2014, for example, the ALDF filed a lawsuit against the Barkworks pet store chain in California. The lawsuit alleged that the chain defrauded customers by selling sick puppies from mills instead of healthy ones from reputable breeders as the stores claimed. The case settled out of court in 2018. The ALDF's legal fights help enforce existing laws that protect animal welfare.

The ALDF also lobbies for new laws. For example, the organization joined with documentary filmmaker Gabriela Cowperthwaite in April 2020 to petition Congress to protect exotic cats. In January 2021, congressmen Mike Quigley (D-IL) and Brian Fitzpatrick (R-PA) reintroduced the Big Cat Public Safety Act in the House of Representatives. If passed, the bill will ban the private ownership of big cats and any physical contact with them, such as petting or feeding. The ALDF also supports legislation at the federal and state level to end animal testing in cosmetics, allow lawyers to represent animals in court proceedings, and make reporting of suspected animal abuse mandatory for veterinarians.

Bella Lack (center) and another young activist speak with Britain's Prince William, Duke of Cambridge, at a 2018 conference on the illegal wildlife trade. Lack uses the energy of youth and the power of social media to raise money for her cause.

Some of the ALDF's biggest fights have been to overturn ag-gag laws that can get in the way of protecting animals. Since 2013, the ALDF has fought laws that make it a crime to document animal cruelty in an undercover investigation. Federal courts have struck down ag-gag laws in four states for violating the First Amendment, but the ALDF remains vigilant. According to the ALDF, "The ability to investigate, document, and publicize corporate agriculture's abuses is imperative both to the well-being of animals across the nation—and to our own health and safety."[20] Despite successes, new ag-gag laws keep popping up like weeds in a field of crops.

In 2020 alone, the ALDF scored twenty-nine victories in court, including shutting down a puppy mill and overturning ag-gag laws in Kansas and North Carolina. As part of a coalition, the ALDF also won legislative victories, including laws to protect pets in California and a law regulating the treatment of farm animals in Colorado.

CHAPTER THREE

The Teen Activist's Tool Kit

A video from late October 2020 shows a handful of protesters outside of an Urban Outfitters store in Austin, Texas. As they pace the sidewalk, the protesters hold signs and chant slogans, a call and response seesaw. "There's no excuse," calls one protester. "For animal abuse,"[21] the others respond. Passersby and customers weave through the small protest line. Some look curious. Others ignore the demonstration. The protest seems haphazard—except for the protesters' signs. They are not marker-scrawled, paint-splashed, do-it-yourself projects. Each white sign sports the same black capitalized font. Two signs have graphic photos of abused animals, and at the bottom of all of them stands the PETA logo. The Austin protest is not haphazard at all. It is one part of PETA's coordinated effort to stop the sale of clothing made from animal-derived materials such as wool, alpaca, and leather. Scroll through the social media of PETA or its youth-led organization, SOS, and you will see similar protests—with the same signs—at Urban Outfitters across the United States and in Europe.

The story of PETA's campaign against Urban Outfitters shows how a large activist organization takes on a multibillion-dollar company. But it also shows the steps and tools activists at all levels use to make change.

A Theory of Change

Activist organizations typically plan their work around a theory of change. A theory of change answers these questions: what change do we seek, and how will we make it happen? There are different models, but a theory of change often specifies an activist's resources, actions, targets, and desired outcomes. It provides a road map to follow and a way to evaluate what worked or did not at the end of a campaign.

To build a theory of change, work backward. Start by identifying your desired outcome. Improving animal welfare is too general. What specific change do you want? Do you want your school to stop animal dissections? Do you want your city to ban the use of wild animals in circuses or your favorite restaurant to use only cage-free eggs? Identify an outcome specific enough that in the end you will know whether you achieved it.

According to reporter Jessica Testa, PETA's campaign against Urban Outfitters started with undercover video shot at an alpaca farm in Peru. The video shows workers slamming frightened alpacas onto tables, restraining them despite their screams, and tearing through their fur with electric clippers. It is disturbing footage that PETA decided to leverage in a new campaign. PETA's desired outcome is eliminating the use of alpaca in clothing.

The next step in building a theory of change is to identify your targets. As activist Yutaka Dirks writes, "Victories don't come by throwing fists in all directions at once, hoping to land a knockout punch by chance alone."[22] Find out who has the power to actually make the change you want to see. If you want to stop dissections, your target might be your science department, your principal, the school board, or all of these, depending on your school's structure. Targets can include individuals, companies,

> "Victories don't come by throwing fists in all directions at once, hoping to land a knockout punch by chance alone."[22]
>
> —Yutaka Dirks, writer and organizer

organizations, agencies, or the legislature, and you can have more than one.

Testa wrote in the *New York Times* about how Urban Outfitters became PETA's target. Even though the mistreatment of alpacas occurred at a farm, PETA needed a target people could identify. Testa reports PETA identified three potential targets: retailers H&M, Gap, and the Urban Outfitters brands, which includes Anthropologie. They are all well-known companies that have power over suppliers like an alpaca farm. They buy materials in large quantities, which make them important customers. PETA also considered these retailers because it thought their customers

Protests are a way for activists to make their views known and garner public attention for their cause. PETA members hoped their protest outside Urban Outfitters stores in London (pictured) and in Austin, Texas, in 2020 would have that effect.

would care about animal welfare, and the companies had been responsive in the past. PETA emailed the potential targets warning they would soon release a video showing abuses at a supplier. After reviewing the footage, H&M and Gap severed ties with the alpaca supplier. Anthropologie did not respond, according to PETA, so the Urban Outfitters brands became the target.

Who has the power to make the change you want? Who can you potentially influence? That is your target. The next step in creating a theory of change is to specify the actions you will use to pressure your targets. Activists have a tool kit of actions, and most campaigns use more than one. Examine some of the tools other activists use and see how you can use them most effectively.

Protest and Petition

Say the word *activism* and certain images of protests may leap to mind. Brightly colored posters splashed with catchy slogans. Songs and chants amplified by megaphones. Energy bouncing through a crowd. In-person protests capture attention, inform, and engage others in a cause. They might change a company's or organization's policies directly, but often protests work indirectly by changing the minds and behaviors of individuals who witness and participate in them or by recruiting new activists. These individuals then exert pressure on a target.

To support PETA's campaign against Urban Outfitters, SOS members helped organize protests outside stores. PETA provides its members with free protest kits that include leaflets and signs. The hope is that if enough customers demand better treatment of alpacas, Urban Outfitters will listen and may concede. At the Austin Urban Outfitters protest, customers still trickled in and out of the store. The action appeared to overwhelm one employee, but most witnesses seemed unfazed. That does not mean the protest failed. Protests can also strengthen commitment to a cause for the people who participate in them.

Besides in-person gatherings, protests can take the form of a letter-writing or phone-calling campaign. SOS, for example, provides a script for people to call a local Urban Outfitters brand store or the corporate headquarters and protest the selling of animal-derived products. Similarly, you can provide call scripts, postcards, or form letters for supporters to contact your target or ask them to craft their own messages.

A petition is a written or electronic request signed by multiple people and delivered to a target with the power to make change. In 2018, teen activist Bella Lack created a petition on Change.org to stop the use of wild animals in British circuses. She gathered over 190,000 signatures. Perhaps partly in response, the British government passed a law in 2019 banning wild animals in circuses.

Protests, letter or phone campaigns, and petitions typically rely on large numbers to make an impact. However, the participants themselves can also matter. The most effective petitions, for example, include signatures of people the target views as important, such as a politician's constituents. A dramatic delivery of a petition or letters might also increase its effectiveness. In 2009, activist organization Avaaz delivered a petition to the World Health Organization (WHO) to request regulation of factory farms. Instead of handing a list of names to a receptionist, Avaaz stuck two hundred cardboard pigs into the field in front of the WHO offices. Each pig represented one thousand petition signers. The creative delivery visually demonstrated the amount of support for the petition and grabbed media attention, spreading the message further. If you do not have large numbers of supporters to participate in a protest, petition, or phone or letter campaigns, work to get influential supporters or add an element of drama to the delivery.

Boycott

Boycotts dot American history time lines all the way back to the Boston Tea Party. A boycott is a refusal to buy a product or participate in an activity as a form of protest. SOS stages protests outside Urban Outfitters stores to discourage customers from buying their animal-derived products. But boycotts can extend beyond a single brand. During the late 1980s, activists called for a boycott of tuna companies using fishing methods harmful to dolphins. Eventually, the largest companies conceded to demands and adopted different fishing techniques. People who choose veganism for animal welfare reasons boycott all animal-derived products. They hope to improve the welfare of animals by putting factory farms out of business.

Research shows that boycotts can make a difference. Boycotts might hit a company's sales directly if enough people stop buying a product, but that is not the only way they work. Business professor Brayden King finds boycotts work primarily by damaging a company's reputation. Companies make concessions to repair damage to their brand and protect profits. Boycotts that capture and sustain media attention have the most potential to damage a company's reputation, according to King.

An online petition drive was the tool of choice for activist Bella Lack when she campaigned for a halt to the use of wild animals, such as this performing elephant, in British circuses.

Raise Funds

Fighting for animal welfare takes money. As activist Nathan Runkle says, "Money is power. It's energy. Used effectively, money has the ability to save and transform lives."[23] From lemonade stands to virtual auctions, people of all ages successfully raise money for causes. Teen activist Zoe Rosenberg raises money to fund her Happy Hen Animal Sanctuary for rescued farm animals. Bella Lack raises funds for Reserva, which buys acres of rain forest to set aside as a reserve. The Gladstone brothers fundraise to support research on the blue-footed booby. The internet bursts with creative ideas for fundraisers that could fit with your goals and resources as well as the interests of your community.

You can raise money for your own organization or for a nonprofit that shares your values and desired outcomes. Fundraising can take place in person or virtually. You can raise money or ask for donations of items, such as pet food, and virtual platforms

A Spectrum of Allies

Who is with me? Who is against me? And, by how much? Activists ask themselves these questions to map a spectrum of allies, an idea Joshua Kahn Russell discusses in the book *Beautiful Trouble*. If you have a change you want to see, try it yourself. Categorize people into one of five different buckets relative to your cause: (1) *active allies* are working to accomplish the same outcome, (2) *passive allies* support your desired outcome but are not working for change, (3) *neutrals* are not engaged at all, (4) *passive opponents* do not support your desired outcome but do not work against you, and (5) *active opponents* do not support your cause and actively work against you.

After you map your allies, try to shift each group by one category. If you want vegan options in the cafeteria, for example, do not try to convince active opponents to boycott the cafeteria until vegan options appear. Focus instead on moving passive allies to take an action, such as lobbying the principal for vegan choices. By shifting allies, you can eventually reach your goal. "Successful movements don't overpower their opponents," write author Greg Satell and political activist Srdja Popovic, "they gradually undermine their opponents' support."

Greg Satell and Srdja Popovic, "How Protests Become Successful Social Movements," *Harvard Business Review*, January 27, 2017. https://hbr.org.

such as GoFundMe or Amazon's Wishlist allow you to reach more people. Check with the organization for which you are fundraising before you begin, and review the policies of online platforms. Communicate the specific goal of your fundraiser and how you will use donations. At the end of the campaign, thank donors and let them know the results.

Lobby

Lobbying is meeting directly with your target to discuss your desired outcome. As members of Beautiful Trouble, a global activist network, say, "Sometimes the quickest way to get what you want is simply to ask for it—in a way that your target . . . can't refuse!"[24] You can lobby lawmakers, such as city council members, or other policy makers, such as school board members.

In 2014, sixth-grader Lila Copeland lobbied her school district, the Los Angeles Unified School District, to put a vegan lunch option on the menu every day in all schools. That is potentially a lot of vegan meals—the district serves 285,000 lunches a day. Copeland and her allies won the opportunity for a trial program at seven schools in 2017, and since then, the program has expanded to other schools in the district.

> "Sometimes the quickest way to get what you want is simply to ask for it—in a way that your target . . . can't refuse!"[24]
>
> —Beautiful Trouble, a global activist network

If you want to lobby, arrange a meeting with your target. Unlike some actions, lobbying does not require a large number of people, but it does require thorough preparation. Know what you want and why you want it. Do not just bring statistics but also stories that help personalize your issue. Ask for something specific, such as a policy change or signature on a petition. Anticipate what your opponent might say and address that argument during the meeting. If you do not know an answer to a question, tell the policy maker you will find out and then follow up. Leave a handout for the policy maker to review later and send a thank you note after the meeting.

Social Media

Social media can enable the mistreatment of animals, but activists also wield its speed and reach to organize and implement change. Social media supports and enhances traditional activism. Get the word out about in-person protests, and then upload photos of it to amplify its impact geographically and across time. Collect hundreds instead of dozens of signatures using an online petition instead of an in-person one. Participate or organize an online boycott or buycott (where you purchase products to support your cause rather than avoid products). To celebrate your birthday or graduation, create an online fundraiser for an animal welfare organization and then use social media to drive traffic to it. You can also connect to other activists online just like you would in person.

Social media also provides entirely new ways to take action. Researchers Jordana J. George and Dorothy E. Leidner categorize digital activism into activities. The most basic activities include what they refer to as clicktivism (liking or following a post or account), metavoicing (sharing, retweeting, or commenting on a post), and creating original content. Critics deride online activism as "slacktivism" because so much of it requires little effort or commitment. But it can still have an impact by quickly spreading information to large numbers of people. The size of the impact depends partly on the characteristics of participants' social networks. Clicktivism, metavoicing, and content creation will have more impact if your social network is large or includes people who do not already actively support animal welfare. Even though clicktivism requires little effort, it may benefit a cause by engaging new people or strengthening the engagement of people who already passively support the cause.

How can you best use social media for making change? Polish your comments and posts. Typos, too much text, or bitter

Make Your Dollars Count

Young Americans spend up to $143 billion a year. How do you know what products support animal welfare?

Some vegan snacks display a vegan-certified logo. If not, check the ingredients. Dairy, eggs, meat, and honey obviously come from animals, but some animal-derived ingredients are less obvious. The food coloring carmine, sometimes listed as *E120* or *Red 4*, comes from beetles. Gelatin, which most gummy bears and marshmallows contain, comes from animal collagen. But Oreos, original Ruffles, and Sour Patch Kids are vegan friendly. No one said eating vegan has to be boring!

If you want to buy personal care products—such as shampoos, soaps, and cosmetics—that have not been tested on animals, look for a certified bunny logo or check the Leaping Bunny, PETA's Bunny Free, or Choose Cruelty Free apps.

Looking for a weekend activity? Before you visit a "sanctuary," check online if it is accredited by the Global Federation of Animal Sanctuaries. Some roadside zoos misleadingly call themselves sanctuaries. Real sanctuaries do not buy, sell, or breed animals; do not let people touch wild animals; and provide enriched habitats.

Whether for snacks, personal care products, or entertainment, your spending choices can make a difference for animals.

comments can make a poor impression. Instead, craft a clear, short message, talk about your personal connection to an issue if you are comfortable doing so, and be specific about how others can get involved. Use hashtags, include photos or other visuals for interest, and highlight the work of other activists.

Lastly, do not forget about traditional media. Traditional news coverage can help you reach others outside your personal social network. Invite the school paper to cover your activities or write an op-ed for a local newspaper. Then use social media to share it widely.

Putting It All Together

Once you have identified a desired outcome, target, and actions, the last piece in a theory of change is resources. Taking action may require money, peers, or new skills. The advice of experienced activists is another resource. Below are three recommendations from activists for making change.

Animal welfare activist Zoe Rosenberg believed the key to achieving a statewide ban on fur sales in California was to start small. Building on one small victory after another can ultimately lead to larger success when fighting for a cause.

Start local and small. Zoe Rosenberg and other activists succeeded in getting California to ban all fur sales in 2019, but they did not start their work at the state level. Instead, they started by passing a ban in Berkeley, California. In a podcast interview, Rosenberg explained that the activists were confident they could get an early win in the city known for its progressive politics. They built momentum as they moved on to bigger cities and then the state. Starting with less controversial issues and on a local level increases your chances of an early victory and can attract others to your cause as you grow.

Make your appeals emotional. No matter what actions you take, you will communicate with targets, supporters, and observers. The most effective messaging does not just inform but also elicits an emotional response. Stories can move people to action. To decrease pet homelessness in your community, for example, consider sharing stories about individual shelter animals. Then link the stories to an action, such as donating money to a low-cost spay and neuter clinic. You can also tell a story about yourself—what motivates you to act? Although outrage is a powerful emotion that may come naturally when fighting for change, be careful. "Anger is an effective mobilizer, but anger without hope is a destructive force," write author Greg Satell and political activist Srdja Popovic. "You need to make an affirmative case with affirmative tactics."[25]

Remain polite, calm, and nonviolent in your interactions. Animal welfare activists fight for better treatment of nonhuman beings. Most would never consider harming human beings or property to get it. There are also practical reasons to stay polite and calm. "Disarm with charm, and maybe your audience will let their guard down long enough to hear what you have to say,"[26] write activists Steven Lambert and Andrew Boyd. Researchers George and Leidner caution against using social media to attack individuals. "There is a very fine line between targeting individuals and such nefarious behaviors as cyberbullying,"[27] they write. Instead, focus your social media activities on positive action and target companies and laws. Violence or insulting a target may alienate people whose support you could otherwise have won. Instead try to connect with people and shift them toward you.

Activists believe that if enough individuals protest, call, petition, and post their ideas about the causes that matter to them, they will succeed. Although you do not have the vast resources of an international activist organization, you can approach your own work with similar tools, strategies, and dedication.

> "Anger is an effective mobilizer, but anger without hope is a destructive force. You need to make an affirmative case with affirmative tactics."[25]
>
> —Greg Satell, author, and Srdja Popovic, political activist

CHAPTER FOUR

Risks and Rights

Lilly Platt moved from the United Kingdom across the North Sea to the Netherlands at age six. One day, soon after her arrival, she took a walk with her grandfather. To practice speaking Dutch, they counted pieces of plastic litter. Within fifteen minutes, Platt had reached ninety-one and the conclusion that she needed to do more than just learn a new language. Thoughtlessly thrown garbage is not only a nuisance, but it also can choke and entangle animals. Some animals mistake synthetic scraps for food, which can harm or even kill them if swallowed. Platt started Lilly's Plastic Pickup to raise awareness. Now at age thirteen, she and her grandfather still gather litter—they collected more than twenty-two thousand pieces in 2019. The teen has also organized community cleanups, has participated in more than one hundred protests, has become a global youth ambassador for Earth.Org, and received multiple awards for her activism.

Picking up trash does not sound controversial, but like other well-known teen activists, Platt faces harassment. "I have received so many comments saying things like 'she's just a child, let the grownups handle this,' or 'this is fake news, how dare you do something like this?'"[28] she told Earth.Org. Platt's mother spends hours every day scrubbing hate off her daughter's social media accounts. The family's computers have been hacked, and Platt's grandfather received a death threat for his support of her work. Detractors accuse the activist's mother of forcing her daughter to campaign against plastic, and even former classmates discouraged Platt.

The cutting criticism and belittling dismissal teen activists like Platt experience can dampen their passion to make change. But nineteen-year-old climate activist Jamie Margolin urges teens to not let hostility sap their energy. Ignore negative messages unless they contain a threat, in which case screenshot and share them with an adult. Margolin also cautions teens to remain professional themselves, not retaliate, and not post inappropriate messages. There is power in taking the moral high ground.

To Bella Lack, the backlash against teen activists proves their effectiveness. "You can see it a bit like a boat," Lack told the hosts of the British television show *This Morning*. "The faster a boat

> "The fact that young activists are receiving quite a lot of opposition is testament to the fact that we're reaching people who haven't been reached before and our message is making people uncomfortable."[29]
>
> —Bella Lack, teen activist

Being in the spotlight, even for a worthy cause, is not always pleasant. Nineteen-year-old climate activist Jamie Margolin (pictured in 2020 with her new book) urges teens to not let hostility sap their energy.

moves in water, the more resistance you feel from the water. . . . The fact that young activists are receiving quite a lot of opposition is testament to the fact that we're reaching people who haven't been reached before and our message is making people uncomfortable."[29] Change is not easy, and some people will resist.

Lack still deals with social media hostility, especially on Twitter, but she has adjusted some over time. Knowing your rights and how to handle situations you might encounter as an activist can give you confidence too. It is important to know what rights you have to protest for animal welfare and what risks you might face in championing such a cause.

Animal Dissection and Your Rights

Some teens find animal dissection fascinating. Others feel overwhelmed by the thought of slicing and splaying an animal killed specifically for a classroom science activity. When science classes dissect animals, they mostly use frogs but also fetal pigs, cats, and other species. These animals come from biology supply companies that source them from breeders, farms, shelters, or the wild. When it comes to dissection, you might not have to pick up a scalpel.

Whether your school can require you to dissect a once-living creature depends on where you attend. Students in California public schools can opt out of school dissections thanks to Jennifer Graham. In 1987, fifteen-year-old Graham refused to dissect a frog for ethical reasons. Her teacher denied Graham's request for an alternative assignment, so Graham and her parents sued the school district. They alleged the school violated Graham's First Amendment rights. Although the case settled out of court, it prompted California to pass legislation in 1988 that gave students the right to choose an alternative. Today, twenty-two states allow public school students to opt out of dissection without penalty. In other states, some individual schools give students an option.

Some animal welfare advocates contend that the choice to opt out is not enough. Instead, they want all dissections of real animals banned. Even when they have a choice, students can feel

A Massachusetts student makes the first cut during dissection of a sheep's brain. In some states, students who object to this practice can opt out; in other states they can request an alternative lesson.

pressured from teachers, peers, or even themselves—falsely believing, for example, a future medical career depends on dissecting an animal. In 2019, the California State Assembly's Committee on Education voted down a proposed bill that would have banned traditional dissection in schools, but activists are not giving up. As alternatives improve, more schools and states could eliminate traditional dissections. No longer just computer programs or apps, today's alternatives include the SynFrog, which gives a complete dissection experience minus the putrid, pickle odor of formaldehyde. Students who dissect the SynFrog slice into knobby, moist skin that covers muscle tissue and squishy organs, but it is all synthetic. If you disagree with your school's dissection policy, consider which tools can help make change and know your rights for using them.

The Right to Protest in School

If you want to protest in a public school against animal dissection, for vegan lunch options, to add animal welfare to the curriculum, or any other animal welfare issue, you have a right to do so. According to the US Supreme Court, students do not "shed

Are There Risks to Going Vegan?

It seems menus, grocery shelves, and celebrities are turning vegan as fast as cheetahs sprint. If you are considering veganism, you should know a few facts.

Eliminating animal-derived products can boost health, but plant-based diets may require some planning. The American Dietetic Association recommends teen vegetarians and vegans watch their intake of calcium, iron, zinc, and vitamins D and B_{12}. Fortified foods or supplements can help, but consult with a doctor and parent before taking the vegan plunge.

Beyond nutritional considerations, you may find it difficult to commit to a vegan diet. According to a study by the Humane Research Council, 84 percent of people who tried a vegan or vegetarian diet abandoned it. For some, finding tasty options proved challenging. More often, vegetarians and vegans reported a lack of social support for their dietary choices. If you want to try veganism, consider who might support or coach you online or in person. Then, go slow. Choose one day of the week or one meal, for example, to eat vegan. Then, build from there.

---

their constitutional rights to freedom of speech or expression at the schoolhouse gate."[30] However, there are limitations. Your actions and expressions cannot substantially disrupt the functioning of the school or violate content-neutral policies. If your activities—making a speech, passing out pamphlets, or fielding a petition—interrupt class time, prevent students or teachers from getting to class, or otherwise interfere with schooling, you can face discipline. Schools can also enforce content-neutral policies on expression. A public school can not only ban hats that display the PETA logo, for example, but can ban all hats. When considering taking action, review the student handbook and plan a protest that does not cause a substantial disruption.

Two court cases have helped clarify what counts as a substantial disruption. In 1965, a group of students, which included siblings John and Mary Beth Tinker, wore black armbands with fluorescent peace signs to school to protest the Vietnam War. Their action did not interrupt class or spark violence, but it did violate a school policy. The school suspended the Tinkers and others who participated. In response, the students sued the district. When the case, *Tinker v. Des Moines Independent Community*

School District, reached the US Supreme Court, the court ruled the school had violated the students' First Amendment rights. Because the students' action did not cause a significant interruption to the school's functioning, it constituted protected expression. The *Tinker* decision established the criterion by which courts still judge school protests today.

Whether a protest counts as a substantial disruption depends not only on the action but also on the context. In 1970, Tennessee high school student Rod Melton wore a jacket with a Confederate flag on the sleeve to school. Staff told Melton he had to take off the jacket with what some people see as a racist symbol or leave. Melton's family sued, alleging the school had violated Melton's First Amendment rights. Although the action—wearing a controversial piece of clothing to school—sounds similar to the *Tinker* case, the context differed. In 1969, racial tensions had led to demonstrations that shut down Melton's school and caused a four-day citywide curfew. In *Melton v. Young*, the Sixth Circuit Court of Appeals ruled that the school did not violate Melton's rights because displaying the Confederate flag could have substantially disrupted school again. Because schools must maintain a safe learning environment, you have fewer rights in school than outside of it.

Other limitations could also curtail your ability to protest at school. You do not have the right to walk out of school during class. If you choose to walk out, the school can discipline you. Schools can conduct locker searches if they are random or school wide, if you give your consent or staff have a reasonable suspicion you violated a policy, or if the locker is school property. If you violate a school cellphone policy, staff can confiscate your phone, but they need your consent or a reasonable suspicion that you violated a school policy before searching its contents. In private schools, the First Amendment will not necessarily protect you. Private schools can further limit students' rights to protest.

Wondering whether schools can discipline you for what you say on social media outside of school? Schools wonder too. Soon, the US Supreme Court will hear the case *Mahoney Area School District v. B.L.* When cheerleader B.L. did not make the senior varsity squad, she posted a curse-filled message one Saturday night on Snapchat. When a cheer coach saw a screenshot of the message, B.L. was suspended from the team for the obscenities and disrespect. The family sued the school, alleging it violated B.L.'s First Amendment rights. The Supreme Court's forthcoming decision will provide guidance to schools and lower courts on whether schools can discipline off campus, online speech. It may come down to whether a post substantially disrupts a school's functioning.

The Right to Protest Outside School

If you want wider reach, take your protest off campus. In public spaces, you have a right to gather peacefully and share your message no matter how unpopular or controversial. The right to protest outside school is one-size-fits-all-ages, but it is not limitless. You typically do not have the right to protest on private property. The police could arrest you for trespassing for doing so. Even in public spaces, you cannot block the flow of pedestrians or traffic, and your right to free speech does not include the right to incite violence. Some local governments require a permit to

Schools have the right to impose limits on protests that take place on campus. Young activists may find that they have greater freedom in off-campus protests but even then, there are limits.

protest or use sound amplification, such as a megaphone, but any local laws must be content neutral; for example, police cannot treat protests against the transport of pigs to slaughter differently than rallies in support of a local politician. In any case, if a protest threatens public safety, police can shut it down.

Pictures can make for compelling evidence in your fight for animal welfare. You have the right to photograph anything in plain sight in a public space, including the police, if it does not interfere with law enforcement. Unlike school staff, police cannot confiscate or search your cell phone without a warrant. Also, police cannot demand you delete something, such as a photograph, from your phone.

> "The right to join with fellow citizens in protest or peaceful assembly is critical to a functioning democracy and at the core of the First Amendment."[31]
>
> —American Civil Liberties Union

If the police stop you while you are demonstrating, stay calm and polite. If it is unclear, ask the officer if you are free to go. Some states have laws that require you to identify yourself, but you do not have to answer other questions posed by police officers or write or sign a statement. You have the right to request a lawyer to be present for questioning. If you do talk, write, or sign something, those things can be used against you in the future. If you think your rights have been violated by the police, gather their identifying information, such as a badge numbers, car number, and what agency they represent. Then talk to your parents or another trusted adult.

Before you organize a protest, check with the local police or government about any rules. You may also want to consult with local veteran activists to understand any unwritten "rules" in your area. Exercise your rights peacefully and according to local laws, and you will not only help improve the lives of animals but also build the muscle of democracy. As the American Civil Liberties Union says, "The right to join with fellow citizens in protest or peaceful assembly is critical to a functioning democracy and at the core of the First Amendment."[31]

Balancing Activism and Teen Life

Activism can invigorate and enrich your life, but it can also wear you down. "In the past year or so I've had barely any time to go out with my friends," Bella Lack told a journalist. "I know at any time I can give [activism] up but I've made a decision now to carry on."[32] Platt and Margolin also juggle school, friends, and family with activism. Yet even rubber bands snap if stretched far enough. So, use small tasks to patch time leaks in the day, Margolin advises. Schedule meetings on a bus ride home or post about an upcoming protest if you arrive early to class. Margolin also suggests making a list of the things you refuse to sacrifice for activism, then prioritize your activities accordingly. Protect your physical and mental health. Get enough sleep, say no when work becomes too much, and find a healthy way to decompress, Margolin urges. Achieving balance between activism and the rest of your life can make you happier and more effective.

The Risk of Unintended Consequences

Banning trade of one vulnerable species might seem like a pure victory, but success sometimes creates new problems. Concern over the decimation of pangolins—scaly, anteater-like mammals—has spurred major conservation efforts. Yet one group of scientists concludes that protecting the pangolin is unintentionally putting the arapaima, an Amazon river fish, at risk. Both animals have diamond-patterned skins used in cowboy boots and other exotic leather accessories. As the supply of pangolin skins has decreased, US customer demand for arapaima skins has increased. If the demand for arapaima does not fall, the vulnerable species could also become threatened.

Substitution happens for other species too. African lion bones have become substitutes for tiger bones in traditional medicines sold in some places in Asia. International agreements regulate trade in tigers more strictly than in African lions. As the African lion population falls, activists urge greater protections for the species.

Successes for one species do not have to lead to losses for another. Squashing consumer demand for exotic skins or big cat bones overall can protect multiple species. Consider how your activism goals fit with the goals of others.

If the mistreatment and suffering of animals incites you, then stand up for animal welfare. You may not know exactly how to start, but start anyway. "The truth is," says Margolin, "no changemaker ever, no youth activist *ever*, has fully known what they were doing. They just learned the best they could, did the best they could with the best intentions, and made the most change they could with what tools they had available to them."[33] Build on the work of other activists, choose strategies from the tool kit, and know your rights and risks. You have the power to speak for the voiceless and defend the vulnerable.

> "No changemaker ever, no youth activist *ever*, has fully known what they were doing. They just learned the best they could, did the best they could with the best intentions, and made the most change they could with what tools they had available to them."[33]
>
> —Jamie Margolin, teen activist

SOURCE NOTES

Introduction: Teens Compelled to Act for Animal Welfare

1. Bella Lack, "Ban the Use of Wild Animals in Circuses Across the UK!," Change.org. www.change.org.
2. Bella Lack, "You Can Solve the Extinction Crisis," TEDx Talks, YouTube, March 4, 2020. www.youtube.com/watch?v=WL2pDmkX9b8.
3. Quoted in Melissa Pandika, "Meet Genesis Butler, the 13-Year-Old Activist with a Plan to Save the Earth," Mic, September 15, 2020. www.mic.com.
4. Zoe Rosenberg, "The Urgency of Animal Liberation: A Teenage Activist's Perspective," in *Voices for Animal Liberation*, ed. Brittany Michelson. New York: Skyhorse, 2020, p. 206.

Chapter One: The Issue Is Animal Welfare

5. Quoted in Lori Rackl, "3 Kid-Friendly Spring Break Getaways Close to Chicago," *Chicago Tribune*, April 6, 2017. www.chicagotribune.com.
6. Quoted in Michelle Gant, "Fairlife Dairy Products Pulled from Store Shelves amid Animal Abuse Controversy," *Today*, June 6, 2019. www.today.com.
7. Quoted in Dave Bangert, "Felony Charge Dropped for Only Ex–Fair Oaks Farms Worker Arrested in Animal Abuse Case," *Lafayette (IN) Journal & Courier*, December 18, 2019. www.jconline.com.
8. Performing Animal Welfare Society, "Meet Owen the Bobcat: Officially Home at PAWS!," July 2020. https://myemail.constantcontact.com/July-Newsletter--Owen-the-bobcat-is-officially-home-at-PAWS-.html?soid=1101778242429&aid=frYV9DO9U6k.
9. Sharon Guynup, "What 'Tiger King' Doesn't Show," *Washington Post*, April 2, 2020. www.washingtonpost.com.
10. Quoted in Paul Vitello, "Pat Derby, Champion of Animal Welfare, Dies at 69," *New York Times*, February 22, 2013. www.nytimes.com.

11. Quoted in American Society for the Prevention of Cruelty to Animals, "Animal Homelessness." www.aspca.org.
12. Quoted in Alicia Parlapiano, "Why Euthanasia Rates at Animal Shelters Have Plummeted," *New York Times*, September 3, 2019. www.nytimes.com.

Chapter Two: The Activists

13. Quoted in Mark Thompson, "An Animal Activist at 15, Nathan Runkle Grows Up to Found Mercy For Animals," *The Edge with Mark Thompson* (podcast), March 2, 2018. www.edge-show.com.
14. Quoted in *Livevegan Podcast*, "Cody Carlson," March 13, 2018. https://livegan.buzzsprout.com.
15. Quoted in People for the Ethical Treatment of Animals, "Students Opposing Speciesism to BBQ a 'Dog,'" March 5, 2020. www.peta.org.
16. Quoted in Jessica Testa, "How PETA Won Its Messy Fight and Took a Seat at the Table," *New York Times*, May 31, 2020. www.nytimes.com.
17. Quoted in Pandika, "Meet Genesis Butler, the 13-Year-Old Activist with a Plan to Save the Earth."
18. Quoted in Reserva: The Youth Land Trust, "Concert for Conservation: Bella Lack," YouTube, July 5, 2020. www.youtube.com/watch?v=KH48Uwh9DYA.
19. Bella Lack, "This Schoolgirl Conservationist Wants You to Be Positive About the Climate Crisis," *Vogue*, March 14, 2020. www.vogue.co.uk.
20. Animal Legal Defense Fund, "Ag-Gag Laws." https://aldf.org.

Chapter Three: The Teen Activist's Tool Kit

21. Quoted in Texas Animal Freedom Fighters, "Activists Crash Urban Outfitters Store," YouTube, October 27, 2020. www.youtube.com/watch?v=30LqWpQdDQQ.
22. Yutaka Dirks, "Principle: Choose Your Target Wisely," in *Beautiful Trouble: A Toolbox for Revolution*, eds. Andrew Boyd and Dave Oswald Mitchell. New York: OR Books, 2016.
23. Nathan Runkle and Gene Stone, *Mercy For Animals: One Man's Quest to Inspire Compassion and Improve the Lives of Farm Animals*. New York: Avery, 2017, p. 281.
24. Beautiful Trouble, "Creative Lobbying." www.beautifultrouble.org.
25. Greg Satell and Srdja Popovic, "How Protests Become Successful Social Movements," *Harvard Business Review*, January 27, 2017. https://hbr.org.

26. Steve Lambert and Andrew Boyd, "Advanced Leafleting," in *Beautiful Trouble: A Toolbox for Revolution*, eds. Andrew Boyd and Dave Oswald Mitchell. New York: OR Books, 2016.
27. Jordana J. George and Dorothy E. Leidner, "From Clicktivism to Hacktivism: Understanding Digital Activism," *Information and Organization,* vol. 29, no. 3, 2019, p. 16. www.sciencedirect.com.

Chapter Four: Risks and Rights

28. Interviewed in Earth.Org, "Lilly Platt: Meet Earth.Org's First Global Ambassador!" https://earth.org.
29. Quoted in *This Morning*, "The London Schoolgirl Who's Been Dubbed the British Greta Thunberg," YouTube, August 6, 2020. www.youtube.com/watch?v=3ZOpnsy-KkQ.
30. Quoted in American Civil Liberties Union, "Students: Know Your Rights! Presentation." www.aclu.org.
31. American Civil Liberties Union, "Rights of Protesters." www.aclu.org.
32. Quoted in Megan Sutton, "Meet the Inspiring Young Women Campaigning to End Period Poverty, Champion Girls' Education and Protect Animal Rights," *Good Housekeeping*, July 3, 2019. www.goodhousekeeping.com.
33. Jamie Margolin, *Youth to Power: Your Voice and How to Use It*. New York: Hachette, 2020, p. 224.

WHERE TO GO FOR IDEAS AND INSPIRATION

Books

Andrew Boyd and Dave Oswald Mitchell, eds., *Beautiful Trouble: A Toolbox for Revolution*. New York: OR Books, 2016.

Jamie Margolin, *Youth to Power: Your Voice and How to Use It*. New York: Hachette, 2020.

Rachel Love Nuwer, *Poached: Inside the Dark World of Wildlife Trafficking*. New York: Da Capo, 2018.

Pete Paxton and Gene Stone, *Rescue Dogs: Where They Come from, Why They Act the Way They Do, and How to Love Them Well*. New York: TarcherPerigee, 2019.

KaeLyn Rich, *Girls Resist! A Guide to Activism, Leadership, and Starting a Revolution*. Philadelphia: Quirk, 2018.

Nathan Runkle and Gene Stone, *Mercy for Animals: One Man's Quest to Inspire Compassion and Improve the Lives of Farm Animals*. New York: Avery, 2017.

Organizations and Other Websites

American Anti-Vivisection Society (AAVS)
https://aavs.org

The AAVS works to stop the use of animals in research, including in product testing, in laboratories, and at schools. The organization's website lists state laws related to dissection in schools and discusses alternatives to using animals in research.

American Civil Liberties Union (ACLU)
www.aclu.org

The ACLU works to protect individuals' constitutional and other legal rights, including the rights to free speech and religious freedom. Besides its work in courtrooms, the ACLU works with legislators and communities to support the rights of students and other groups. Its website is a resource for understanding your legal rights inside and outside of school.

American Society for the Prevention of Cruelty to Animals (ASPCA)
www.aspca.org

The ASPCA is a nonprofit best known for its work on behalf of companion animals. Its website provides information about the threats to companion animal welfare, suggestions for getting involved, and advice about adopting and caring for animals.

Animal League Defense Fund (ALDF)
https://aldf.org

The ALDF improves animal welfare using the legal system, either by taking legal action based on existing laws or by lobbying for new ones. The ALDF's website provides information about the issues facing all types of animals, summaries of their current and past cases, and overviews of recently introduced state and federal bills.

Humane Society of the United States
www.humanesociety.org

The Humane Society of the United States is a nonprofit organization that works to improve the lives of all kinds of animals, from alpacas to zebras. Its website includes overviews of the issues and lists current state laws related to puppy mills, animal fighting, and farm animals.

Reserva: The Youth Land Trust
https://reservaylt.org

Reserva is a nonprofit foundation that organizes youth in conservation. Currently, Reserva is raising funds to protect land in the Ecuadorian rain forest. The organization's website includes field notes from explorations of the Dracula Youth Reserve, ideas for youth interested in fundraising for the cause, and opportunities for youth to protect the rain forest through letters rather than dollars.

Students Opposing Speciesism (SOS)
https://sos.peta.org

Launched in 2020, SOS is a youth-led group within PETA for people ages thirteen to twenty-four. SOS's website provides information on animal welfare issues, shows how to get involved, and gives youth interested in animal welfare the opportunity to connect with others in their area.

YouthInFront
www.youthinfront.org

This website is a collection of resources, including numerous videos, that address the frequently asked questions of activist-minded youth. The website provides advice on the methods, risks, and rights of youth protesters fighting for any cause.

News Articles

Rene Ebersole, "The Black-Market Trade in Wildlife Has Moved Online, and the Deluge Is 'Dizzying,'" *National Geographic*, December 18, 2020. www.nationalgeographic.com.

Alaa Elassar, "A Florida High School Is the First in the World to Provide Synthetic Frogs for Students to Dissect," CNN, November 30, 2019. https://edition.cnn.com/.

Linda Givetash, "Young Female Climate Activists Face Hateful Abuse Online. This Is How They Cope," NBC News, November 10, 2019. www.nbcnews.com.

Sharon Guynup, "What 'Tiger King' Doesn't Show," *Washington Post*, April 2, 2020. www.washingtonpost.com.

Andrew Jacobs, "Is Dairy Farming Cruel to Cows?," *New York Times*, December 29, 2020. www.nytimes.com.

Greg Satell and Srdja Popovic, "How Protests Become Successful Social Movements," *Harvard Business Review*, January 27, 2017. https://hbr.org.

Documentaries

Gabriella Cowperthwaite, dir., *Blackfish*. Atlanta: CNN Films, 2013.

Apps

Leaping Bunny
www.leapingbunny.org

This free app identifies cosmetics, household items, and personal care products made without animal testing and certified as cruelty free by Leaping Bunny. A user can scan barcodes or search by brand name or product type while shopping.

Shopwell
www.innit.com/shopwell

This free app helps vegetarians or vegans identify products consistent with their dietary choices. Set up a profile as a vegan, for example, scan the barcode on a food product, and the app will show whether it contains any animal-derived ingredients. The app can also help identify products consistent with other dietary issues, such as food allergies.

INDEX

Note: Boldface page numbers indicate illustrations.

activists and activism
  backlash against, 44–46
  boycotts by, 36–37
  and finding and developing allies, 38
  finding balance in life of, 52
  fundraising for, 38–39
  lobbying and, 39–40
  organizations for, 30
    American Civil Liberties Union, 51
    American Society for the Prevention of Cruelty to Animals, 15, 17, 27–28
    Animal Hero Kids, 27
    Animal Legal Defense Fund, 27, 30–31
    Animal Recovery Mission, 9–10, 27
    Avaaz, 36
    Blue Feet Foundation, 24
    Earth.Org, 44
    Genesis for Animals, 26
    Global Federation of Animal Sanctuaries, 41
    Humane Society of the United States, 18
    Mercy for Animals, 22–23
    People for the Ethical Treatment of Animals, 23–25, 26
    Rainforest Trust, 29
    Reserva, 29, 38
    Students Opposing Speciesism, 23–24, **25**, 35–37
  theory of change and, 33–34
  Wings of Rescue, 28
  Youth Climate Save, 26
  in the past, 5, 48–49
  petitions by, 36, **37**
  protests by
    campaign against Urban Outfitters and, 32, 33, **34**, 34–36
    at National Collegiate Athletic Association's football championship game, 7
    types of, 35–36
  steps to achieving goals of, 42–43
  undercover, 9, 13, 22
  unintended consequences and, 51
ag-gag laws, 13, 31
Alaska Zoo, 15
alpaca farms, 33, 34, 35
American Civil Liberties Union, 51
American Dietetic Association, 48
American Society for the Prevention of Cruelty to Animals (ASPCA), 15, 17, 27–28
animal dissection, 46–47, **47**
Animal Hero Kids, 27
Animal Legal Defense Fund (ALDF), 27, 30–31
Animal Recovery Mission (ARM), 9–10, 27
Animal Welfare Act
  animals exempt from, 10, 16
  standards for breeders in, 19
Anthropologie, 34, 35
anticruelty laws, farm animals excepted from, 8, 10, 16
antifur campaign, 25, 42, **42**
arapaima, 51
Association of Zoos and Aquariums, 15
Avaaz, 36

bears in captivity, 14

Beautiful Trouble (Russell), 38
Bershadker, Matt, 17–18, 20
Big Cat Public Safety Act (proposed), 30
Blue Feet Foundation, 24
blue-footed boobies, 24, 38
bobcats in captivity, 14
boycotts, 36–37
Boyd, Andrew, 43
Butler, Genesis, 4, 5, **6**, 26

California, 42, **42**, 46–47
capuchins in captivity, 14
change, theory of, 33–34
chickens
    broiler, on factory farms, 11
    egg-laying, on factory farms, 10–11, 12, **12**
Christian Science Monitor, 24
circus animals, 4, 36
clicktivism, 40
climate change and factory farms, 26
companion animals. *See* pets
consumerism
    boycotts and, 36–37
    certification of products and, 41
    spending power of teenagers and, 6
Copeland, Lila, 39
Couto, Richard, 10
Cowperthwaite, Gabriela, 30
cows on factory farms, 10, 11, **11**, 12

Daly, Lizzie, 29
Derby, Patricia, 17
dog fighting, 15

Earth.Org, 44
elephants, 15, 29
Endangered Species Act, 16
exotic animals. *See* wild animals

factory farms
    animals on, 10–11, **11**, 12, **12**
    Avaaz campaign against, 36
    climate change and, 26
    locations of, 26
    profit maximized on, 12
Fairlife milk, 9, 27

Fair Oaks Farms (Indiana), 9, 27
farm animals
    on factory farms, 10–11, **11**, 12, **12**
    laws exempting, 8, 10, 16
    laws to improve welfare of, 23
    sanctuaries for, 38
    and practice of thumping pigs, 21
First Amendment rights
    ag-gag laws and, 13, 31
    in public spaces off school campuses, **50**, 50–51
    in school, 47–49, **50**
    social media outside of school and, 49–50
Fitzpatrick, Brian, 30
free speech. *See* First Amendment rights
fundraising, 38–39
fur ban in California, 42, **42**

Galápagos Islands, 24
Gap, 34, 35
Gates, Krystal, 24
Genesis for Animals, 26
George, Jordana J., 40, 43
Gladstone, Matthew, 24
Gladstone, Will, 24
Global Federation of Animal Sanctuaries, 41
Graham, Jennifer, 46
Guynup, Sharon, 16

habitat destruction, 29
H&M, 34, 35
Happy Hen Animal Sanctuary, 38
homelessness, 5
Humane Research Council, 48
Humane Society of the United States, 18

Instagram, 24
Iowa, 13

King, Brayden, 37
kitten farms, 18

Lack, Bella, **31**

on backlash against teen activists,
  45–46
frustration of, 5
petitions, 36
on place of activism in her life, 52
Reserva and, 29, 38
use of social media by, 4, 28–30
Lahey, Kevin, 22
Lambert, Steven, 43
laws
  ag-gag, 13, 31
  Animal Welfare Act, 10, 16
  British, banning wild animals in
    circuses, 4, 36
  consumer protection, 27
  Endangered Species Act, 16
  to improve welfare of farm animals,
    23
  proposed, 30
  state, 16–17
Leidner, Dorothy E., 40, 43
Liebman, Matthew, 13
lobbying, 39–40

Mahoney Area School District v. B.L.,
  49–50
March For Our Lives, 5
Margolin, Jamie
  book written by, 45, **45**
  on finding balance in life of activism,
    52
  on learning by doing, 53
media, traditional, 41
Melton, Rod, 49
Melton v. Young, 49
Mercy For Animals, 22–23
metavoicing, 40

National Collegiate Athletic
  Association's football championship
  game, 7
Nazi atrocities, 5
New York Times (newspaper), 20, 25, 34

pangolins, 52
Parlapiano, Alicia, 17
People for the Ethical Treatment of
  Animals (PETA)

campaign against Urban Outfitters,
  32, 32, 33, **34**, 34–36
Students Opposing Speciesism and,
  23–25
Young Animal Activist of the Year
  award, 26
Performing Animal Welfare Sanctuary
  (PAWS), 14, 15, 17
petitions, 36, **37**
pets
  annual spending on, 8
  American Society for the Prevention
    of Cruelty to Animals and, 17,
    27–28
  breeding of, 18–19, 20, 30
  euthanasia rates of, 17
  in shelters, 17–18, **19**
  social media and, 20
  stores selling, 19–20, 30
Platt, Lilly, 44–45, 52
pollution from factory farms, 26
Popovic, Srdja, 38, 43
protests
  and campaign against Urban
    Outfitters, 32, 33, **34**, 34–36
  at National Collegiate Athletic
    Association's football
    championship game, 7
  in schools, 47–49
  types of, 35–36
puppy mills, 18–19, 20, 30

Quigley, Mike, 30

Rainforest Trust, 29
Reiman, Tracy, 25
Reserva: The Youth Land Trust, 29,
  38
roadside zoos, 15–16
Rosenberg, Zoe, 4
  California fur ban and, 42, **42**
  Happy Hen Animal Sanctuary and,
    38
  protest by, during National Collegiate
    Athletic Association's football
    championship, 7
Runkle, Nathan, 21–23, **23**, 38
Russell, Joshua Kahn, 38

sanctuaries
   accreditation of, 41
   Happy Hen Animal Sanctuary, 38
   Performing Animal Welfare
      Sanctuary, 14, 15, 17
Satell, Greg, 38, 43
shelters
   American Society for the Prevention
      of Cruelty to Animals and, 27–28
   partnering with stores, 19–20
   sources of animals in, 17–18, **19**
Sir Paul McCartney Young Veg
   Advocate award, 26–27
slacktivism, 40
social media
   backlash against activists on, 44–46
   Lack on, 4, 28–29
   methods for using, 40–41
   People for the Ethical Treatment of
      Animals on, 25
   pets and, 20
   promotion of veganism on, 26
   raising money on, 24, 38–39
   schools and free speech on, outside
      of school, 49–50
   Students Opposing Speciesism on,
      24
speciesism, 24
Students Opposing Speciesism (SOS),
   23–24, **25**, 35–37
SynFrog, 47

TEDx talks, 26, 29
Testa, Jessica, 33, 34
theory of change, 33–34
tigers in captivity, 13, 15–16
Tinker, John, 48–49
Tinker, Mary Beth, 48–49
Tinker v. Des Moines Independent
   Community School District, 48–49
tuna boycott, 37

United Kingdom, 4, 36
Urban Outfitters, 32, 33, **34**, 34–37

US Department of Agriculture (USDA),
   11
US Supreme Court, 47–49

vegan diet (veganism)
   animal abuse and, 9
   Butler on, 26
   and certifying food and personal
      care products as animal free, 41
   lobbying for, 39
   nutritional considerations for, 48
   popularity of, 48
Vegetarian Resource Group, 8
VegNews, 13
videos
   of Fair Oaks Farms, 9, 27
   laws against, 13
   by Mercy For Animals activists, 22
   purpose of, 22–23
   Urban Outfitters, 33
   on YouTube, 29
Vietnam War, 48–49

whistleblowers, laws against, 13
wild animals
   breeding of, 16
   British law banning, in circuses,
      36
   in captivity, 13–14
   habitat destruction and, 29
   trade of, 16–17
   unintended consequences of
      activism on, 52
   See also laws
William (Duke of Cambridge, prince of
   England), **31**
Wings of Rescue, 28
World Health Organization (WHO), 36

Young Animal Activist of the Year
   award, 26
Youth Climate Save, 26

zoos, 15–16

PICTURE CREDITS

Cover: behzad moloud/Shutterstock.com

6: Leonard Ortiz/ZUMA Press/Newscom
11: Wang Ping Xinhua News Agency/Newscom
12: Guitar photographer/Shutterstock.com
19: Celiafoto/Shutterstock.com
23: Associated Press
25: Romy Arroyo Fernandez/ZUMA Press/Newscom
31: Avalon.red/Newscom
34: Keith Mayhew/Landmark Media Landmark Media/Newscom
37: MediaProduction/iStock
42: Whiteaster/Shutterstock.com
45: Associated Press
47: Associated Press
50: Jacob Lund/Shutterstock.com

ABOUT THE AUTHOR

Jennifer Stephan writes nonfiction books and articles for tweens and teens. Her work explores how people change and are changed by the communities and times in which they live. She earned a doctorate in human development and social policy from Northwestern University and has worked as an education policy researcher. She lives outside Chicago with her husband, daughters, and a cat named Pumpkin Pie.